Really and Truly

Written by Émilie Rivard
Illustrations by Anne–Claire Delisle

© 2011 Owlkids Books Inc.
10 Lower Spadina Avenue, Suite 400, Toronto, Ontario M5V 2Z2
www.owlkids.com

Text © 2011 Émilie Rivard
Illustrations © 2011 Anne-Claire Delisle
Translation © 2011 Sarah Quinn

Published in Quebec under the title *Vrai de vrai, papi?* © 2011
Bayard Canada Livres Inc., Montreal (Quebec), Canada
www.bayardlivres.ca

Distributed in Canada by University of Toronto Press
5201 Dufferin Street, Toronto, Ontario M3H 5T8

Distributed in the United States by Publishers Group West
1700 Fourth Street, Berkeley, California 94710

Library and Archives Canada Cataloguing in Publication

Rivard, Émilie, 1983-
[Vrai de vrai, papi?. English]
    Really and truly / written by Émilie Rivard ; illustrated by Anne-Claire Delisle ; translated by Sarah Quinn.

Translation of: Vrai de vrai, papi?
Issued also in electronic format.
ISBN 978-1-926973-40-1

    I. Delisle, Anne-Claire II. Quinn, Sarah III. Title. IV. Title:
Vrai de vrai, papi?. English.

PS8635.I83V7213 2012   jC843'.6   C2011-907645-4

Library of Congress Control Number: 2011943507

Canadian Heritage   Patrimoine canadien

Canada Council for the Arts   Conseil des Arts du Canada

Canadä

Ontario
Ontario Media Development Corporation
Société de développement de l'industrie des médias de l'Ontario

ONTARIO ARTS COUNCIL
CONSEIL DES ARTS DE L'ONTARIO

We acknowledge the financial support of the Canada Council for the Arts, the Ontario Arts Council, the Government of Canada through the Canada Book Fund (CBF) and the Government of Ontario through the Ontario Media Development Corporation's Book Initiative for our publishing activities.

Manufactured by C&C Joint Printing Co., (Guangdong) Ltd.
Manufactured in Shenzhen, China, in December 2011
Job #201111633

A   B   C   D   E   F

Publisher of Chirp, chickaDEE and OWL
www.owlkids.com

For Noé, who is better at making grandpas smile than anyone I know!
Émilie

In memory of Mom and Dad
Anne-Claire

When I was little, my grandpa
used to tell me lots of stories.

I loved all the adventures he
dreamed up for me.

Some days he'd say, "Charlie, did I ever tell you about the pirate who lives in my attic?"

"Sometimes when I'm reading
my newspaper, I can hear his
wooden leg bumping up
against an old treasure chest.
Knock, knock, knock…
Really and truly, Charlie!"

The next day he'd say, "Charlie, remember the pirate I was telling you about? Well, he has a friend, an old witch. She lives in my shed back there in the yard."

"If you look carefully, you can see her toad hopping around the garden and her bat hanging from the clothesline. Really and truly, Charlie!"

When I'd ask Grandpa about the hole
in the living room floor, he'd say,
"Oh that! That's because there's a gnome
who lives in my basement."

"On rainy days when water comes in the window, the little
guy has to climb up a ladder so his feet don't get wet. Rainy
day after rainy day, he eventually made that hole in my floor
to escape from the basement. Really and truly, Charlie!"

Now that I'm older, Grandpa doesn't tell stories anymore.
He doesn't remember the pirate or the witch or the gnome.
An awful disease has eaten up his memory and his words.
It has even swallowed up his smile.

This week, just like every week, I'm visiting
Grandpa with my mom and dad.

When we walk into his room, he doesn't
even turn around. The cars driving by outside are
more interesting than we are.

If I don't answer my mom when she talks to me,
I get in trouble right away. But she just lets Grandpa
look out the window. I can tell it makes her sad.

Suddenly, a story that Grandpa used to tell me pops into my head. I turn to him and say, "It is I, Akimoto Kata! I am a great warrior, the best ninja in all of Japan."

"I have a secret weapon. I freeze my enemies by making them drink a special tea. Do you know what the secret ingredient is?"

Grandpa doesn't answer.
I tug gently on his ear and
say, "It is…the right ear of a
sourpuss! Really and truly!"

Right away Grandpa turns and
looks at us. I think he almost believes me!
Thanks to my story, he isn't looking at the
cars outside anymore.

The next week, we go back to see Grandpa. A nice lady puts down a tray of food in front of him. Grandpa pokes at a meatball with his fork and mashes up his potatoes. He plays with his food without even eating a single bite.

When I was little, Grandpa always used to tell me a special story when I refused to eat. It just might work...

So I say, "I am Mansa, the most famous hunter in all of Africa. I hunt only the finest, most tender, most delicious gazelles in the whole world, and I caught this one just for you! Really and truly! I trekked through the bush and fought thousands of lions, and you don't even want to try a bite?"

At first, Grandpa looks surprised. He raises an eyebrow.
Then he pokes his fork into a meatball and pops it into
his mouth. Little by little, he eats everything on his plate.

During the whole next week, I can't stop thinking about Grandpa. I try to come up with the very best story…the one that will make him smile again.

On visiting day, I walk right up close to Grandpa and say, "It is me, the Great Albini! The best magician in the world! I have come a long way to perform my most amazing magic trick just for you."

"I am going to make something appear out of thin air right before your eyes…something extraordinary! Really and truly!"

I wave my hands while I say the magic words:

Abracadabra super spaghetti,
Abracadabra rainbow confetti,
The Great Albini is here to say,
Come out, smile, come out and stay!

I look behind Grandpa's ear, but I don't find what I'm looking for.

I check in Mom's purse.
Still nothing.

I search my pocket...
Got it!

I show Grandpa the happy face on the palm of my hand and I say, "Here it is! I found your smile! Now you can have it back!"

I put my hand on Grandpa's scratchy cheek.
Suddenly his face fills with happiness.
His awful disease didn't eat up his smile.
It was just hidden away, deep down in the
bottom of his heart.

A few days later, I run into Grandpa's
room before Mom or Dad.
I can't wait to make him smile!

Grandpa slowly opens his mouth and says,
"Who are you?"

Mom answers, "It's Charlie, your grandson."

He frowns down at me with his enormous eyebrows.
"I don't know anyone called Charlie," he says.

I'm happy that Grandpa is finally talking.
But he doesn't recognize me, and that makes me sad.

Then I get an idea.

"That's because my real name is Claudio Esperanzo, the magician elf! I disguised myself so you wouldn't recognize me!"

Grandpa bursts out laughing!

For a moment, his awful disease seems to have hidden itself away in the pirate's treasure chest or the witch's cauldron or under the gnome's pointy hat.

At my next visit, maybe Grandpa
will pout, maybe he won't want to eat or talk.
Maybe he won't even know who I am again.
But from now on, I have Grandpa's magical power.
The power to find the right story to make him smile.

Really and truly!